The Twelve Laws of Santa Claus

EMILY,

MAY PEACE, LOVE AND JOY
BE YOURS EVERY DAY
OF THE YEAR.

The Twelve Laws of Santa Claus

by
Christopher Hogan Lay

for everyone, of any age
wishing to believe...

Gather 'round everyone.
Get comfortable, I insist.
I have a story to tell,
You won't want to miss.

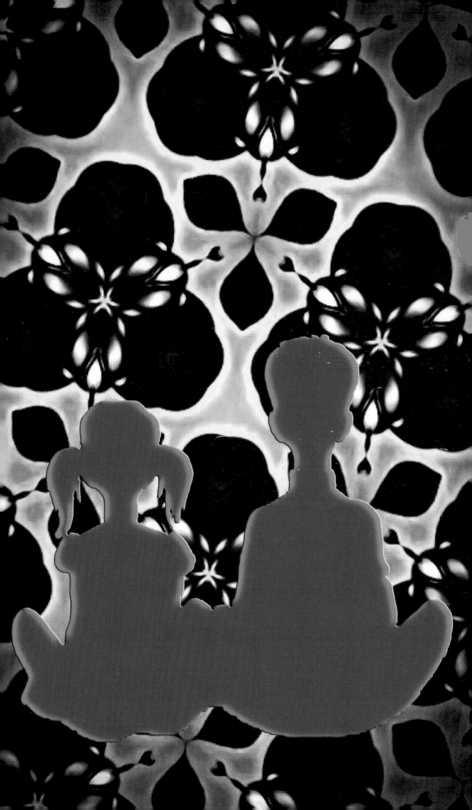

Kris Kringle wants Christmas Spirit,
For the world all year round.
And he needs every one of us,
To help lift it off the ground.

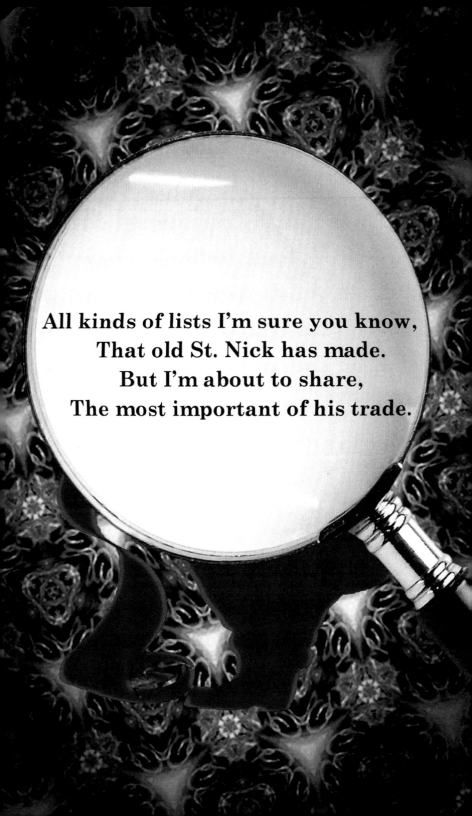

All kinds of lists I'm sure you know,
That old St. Nick has made.
But I'm about to share,
The most important of his trade.

The
Twelve Laws
of
Santa Claus

Law Twelve

12

Love

Santa's list begins with love,
Counting down from twelve to one.
Love yourself first before,
Sharing your heart with anyone.

Law Eleven

11

Be Kind

To be kind, says Santa,
Is such a wonderful thing.
Kindness to each other,
Can ease life's hurts and stings.

Law Ten

10

Choose Good

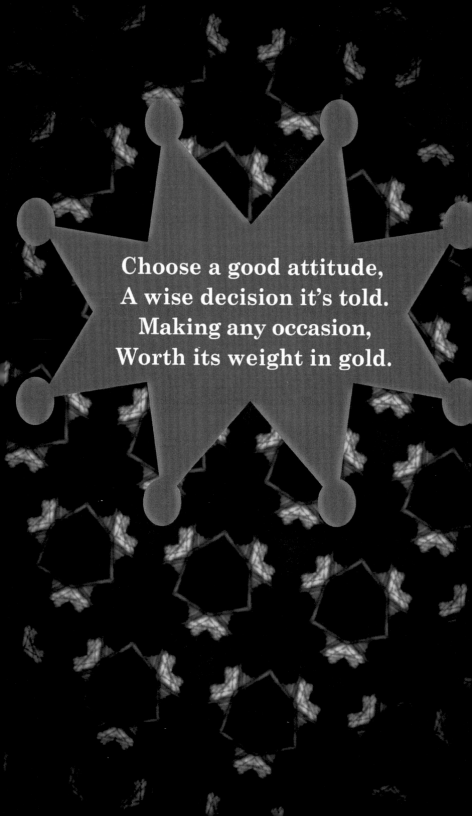

Choose a good attitude,
A wise decision it's told.
Making any occasion,
Worth its weight in gold.

Law Nine

9

Play

Play! Make a game,
Out of any old chore.

Enjoy what you're doing,
And it's never a bore.

Be Grateful

To be thankful or grateful,
Is Law Number Eight.
Doing so helps you feel,
Full and great.

Law Seven

Imagine

Imagine all things possible.
Creativity is key.
To show where life may take you,
And who you'll grow to be.

Law Six

Bring Peace

Be silent.
Shhh! Listen!

There's no need to shout.
When you are still and peaceful,
You will never miss out.

Law Five

Learn

Grow from your mistakes.
Learn new things each day.
If you don't succeed,
Try another way.

Law Four

4

Be Patient

Patience is a virtue.
Bet you've heard that before.
Waiting gets us ready,
For what the future has in store.

Give

Give a gift of yourself.
Help out! Lend a hand.
Santa's Law Number Three,
Keeps you high in demand.

2

Bring Joy

Bring joy! Make friends.
Brighten up someone's day.
Peace, Love and Joy:
That's the Santa Claus way.

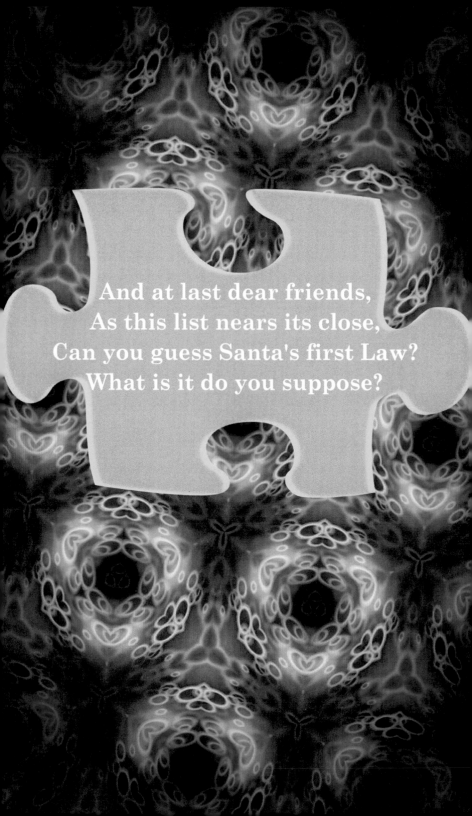

And at last dear friends,
As this list nears its close,
Can you guess Santa's first Law?
What is it do you suppose?

Law One

1

Believe

Believe in yourself,
There's no stopping you.
Believe in your dreams,
And Santa Claus too.